North Vanco

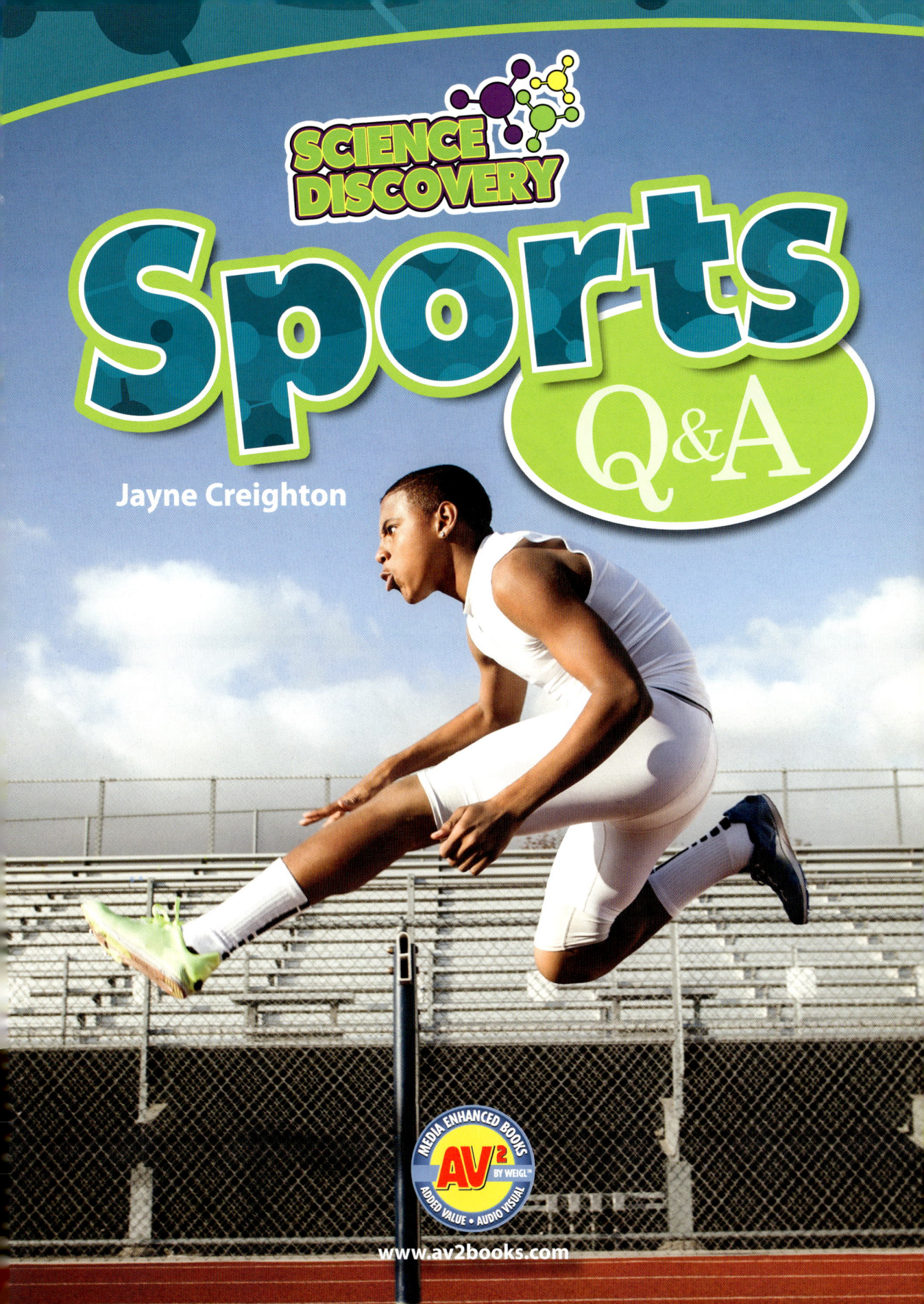

# SCIENCE DISCOVERY

# Sports

## Q&A

Jayne Creighton

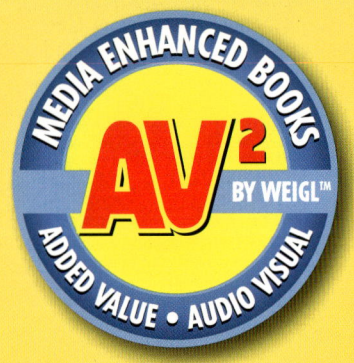

AV² provides enriched content that supplements and complements this book. Weigl's AV² books strive to create inspired learning and engage young minds in a total learning experience.

## Your AV² Media Enhanced books come alive with...

**Audio**
Listen to sections of the book read aloud.

**Key Words**
Study vocabulary, and complete a matching word activity.

**Video**
Watch informative video clips.

**Quizzes**
Test your knowledge.

**Embedded Weblinks**
Gain additional information for research.

**Slide Show**
View images and captions, and prepare a presentation.

**Try This!**
Complete activities and hands-on experiments.

**... and much, much more!**

Go to **www.av2books.com**, and enter this book's unique code.

## BOOK CODE

**F345413**

AV² **by Weigl** brings you media enhanced books that support active learning.

Published by AV² by Weigl
350 5th Avenue, 59th Floor
New York, NY 10118
Websites: www.av2books.com    www.weigl.com

Library of Congress Control Number: 2013953158

ISBN 978-1-4896-0696-9 (hardcover)
ISBN 978-1-4896-0697-6 (softcover)
ISBN 978-1-4896-0698-3 (single-user eBook)
ISBN 978-1-4896-0699-0 (multi-user eBook)

Printed in the United States of America, in North Mankato, Minnesota
1 2 3 4 5 6 7 8 9 0  18 17 16 15 14

042014
WEP301113

Project Coordinator  Aaron Carr
Designer  Mandy Christiansen

Every reasonable effort has been made to trace ownership and to obtain permission to reprint copyright material. The publishers would be pleased to have any errors or omissions brought to their attention so that they may be corrected in subsequent printings.

Photo Credits
Weigl acknowledges Getty Images as its primary photo supplier for this title.

# Contents

AV² Book Code ...................................... 2

What Is a Sport? .................................... 4

How Do Muscles Affect Running? .............. 6

What Happens When
     People Exercise? ............................... 8

Why Warm Up Before Exercising? ............. 10

Are Children More Likely
     to Get Injured? ................................ 12

What Are Extreme Sports? ......................... 14

What Are Human Machines? ...................... 16

How Does Equipment Help Results? ....... 18

How Does Clothing
     Affect Performance? .................................. 20

Are Sports Drinks Better Than Water? ..... 22

What Are Steroids? ....................................... 24

What Role Do Animals Play in Sports? .... 26

How Does a Bike Stay Upright? ................ 28

How Do Surfers Stay
     on Their Boards? ......................................... 30

Do Ice Skaters Become Dizzy
     When They Spin? ......................................... 32

How Does a Pitcher Outsmart
     a Batter? ......................................... 34

How Can a Karate Chop
     Break a Board? ............................................ 36

What Makes a Boomerang Return? ......... 38

Why Do Balls Bounce? .................................. 40

Putting It All Together ................................. 42

Sports Careers ................................................. 44

Young Scientists at Work ........................... 45

Quiz ...................................................................... 46

Key Words/Index .......................................... 47

Log on to www.av2books.com ................. 48

# What Is a Sport?

A sport is a game or activity that is governed by a set of rules or customs. In many sports, people or teams compete against each other. The physical abilities of each competitor determine if he or she will be good at the game. Science is all around us when we take part in sports. When you ride a bicycle or play soccer, you use the laws of **physics**. When you flex your muscles, **biology** is involved. When you work out and get thirsty, **chemistry** is in action. Chemical changes in your body tell you that you need water. Being a good athlete takes more than talent. It also takes science.

## How Scientists Use Inquiry to Answer Questions

When scientists try to answer a question, they follow the process of scientific inquiry. They begin by making observations and asking questions. Then, they propose an answer to their question. This is called the hypothesis. The hypothesis guides scientists as they research the issue. Research can involve performing experiments or reading books on the subject. When their research is finished, scientists examine their results and review their hypothesis. Often, they discover that their hypothesis was incorrect. If this happens, they revise their hypothesis and go through the process of scientific inquiry again.

# Process of Scientific Inquiry

## Observation

Many areas of science are related to success in sports. Different sports illustrate different scientific facts or principles.

## Have You Answered the Question?

The cycle of scientific inquiry never truly ends. For example, once you know about the positive effects of a workout for basketball players, you may need to ask, "Is this workout effective for soccer players, too?"

## Research

For many years, scientists have studied the connection between science and sports. They do this by asking questions such as, "Why are some people better at sports than others?"

## Results

The results of an experiment tell scientists if their hypothesis is correct. For example, scientists may find that certain exercises lead to better results for basketball players. Often, an experiment leads to more questions, more hypotheses, and more experiments.

## Hypothesis

Scientists may hypothesize that athletes can improve their performance by changing their workouts.

## Experiment

To test a hypothesis, scientists perform experiments. For example, they have studied how different muscles in the body affect athletes' speed.

# How Do Muscles Affect Running?

Muscles are attached to bones and make the bones move. Tiny **cells** called muscle fibers make up people's muscles. There are two different kinds of muscle fibers. These are called slow-twitch and fast-twitch fibers.

Slow-twitch fibers, which are dark in color, are used when a person is doing an **endurance** sport, such as long-distance running, cycling, or gymnastics. These fibers have the ability to keep working steadily over a long period of time. Fast-twitch fibers, which are pale in color, are able to contract very rapidly. They are used when the body needs to move quickly for a short time, such as while playing football or sprinting. However, fast-twitch fibers tire easily.

People are born with different amounts of slow-twitch and fast-twitch muscle fibers. Scientists have taken samples of muscle **tissue** from different athletes. Studies have found that sprinters' leg muscles consist of about 65 percent fast-twitch fibers. In contrast, long distance runners' muscles consist of about 75 percent slow-twitch fibers. These differences partly explain why sprinters can run fast for short distances only, and marathon runners run more slowly for long distances.

Muscle fibers are not the only reason for differences in speed. Strength, natural ability, and endurance also play vital roles. Strength and endurance can be improved with training, but the kinds of muscle fiber in a person's body stay the same.

⌄ Speed and a quick start are important for offensive football players such as running backs. They are also important for defensive players, who try to stop the running back from moving down the field.

# Digging Deeper

## Your Challenge!

Muscle fibers are classified as slow-twitch or fast-twitch. To dig deeper into the issue:

Make a two-column chart. On one side, list three activities best performed by slow-twitch fibers. On the other side, list three activities best performed by fast-twitch fibers. These should be different from the activities you have already read about here.

## Summary

Slow-twitch fibers are best for running long distances. Fast-twitch fibers are best for running fast for short distances.

## Further Inquiry

Exercise cannot change muscle fibers, but it affects muscles in other ways. Maybe we should ask:

### What happens when people exercise?

# What Happens When People Exercise?

Muscles generally need oxygen to use food energy stored in the body. This energy allows muscles to work, so that people can run, lift objects, or do other activities. During exercise, muscles use more oxygen than when a person is resting.

Oxygen comes from the air people breathe. It travels throughout the body in the blood. During exercise, a person's lungs must breathe deeper and faster. When muscles work steadily for long periods of time, they must have a constant supply of oxygen. Exercise that involves such steady activity is called aerobic exercise.

⌄ Scientists have found that children who exercise may have better health as adults.

▲ Exercise helps the body produce chemicals that can give people a sense of happiness.

Without using oxygen, muscles can get some energy from sugar stored in the body. This energy allows muscles to perform short, intense bursts of activity. When muscles work for short times without using oxygen, this is called anaerobic activity. If muscles work without oxygen, a substance called lactic acid builds up in them. This acid causes muscles to become sore.

When people exercise, their muscles produce heat. If the body becomes too hot, it may stop working properly. An organ in the brain called the hypothalamus helps the body maintain a steady temperature of about 98.6° Fahrenheit (37° Celsius). If the hypothalamus senses that the body is becoming too warm, it sends signals to sweat glands under the skin to release moisture. When people sweat, the moisture is warm, just like the body. This sweat **evaporates** into the air. As it evaporates, it removes some of the body's excess heat. Sweating is the best way for the body to cool itself.

# Digging Deeper

## Your Challenge!

People breathe harder and sweat during exercise. Their bodies respond to activity, whether aerobic or anaerobic. To dig deeper into the issue:

Research the type of activity most common in different sports. List three sports in which athletes mostly engage in aerobic activity and three sports in which athletes do more anaerobic activity.

## Summary

When people exercise, they breathe more deeply to take in more oxygen. Their bodies become warmer, and they sweat to cool down their bodies.

## Further Inquiry

Exercise changes how the body functions. Maybe we should ask:

### Why warm up before exercising?

# Q&A

## Why Warm Up Before Exercising?

It is helpful to warm up before playing a sport or starting a vigorous activity. To warm up, people do a short period of exercise that is not too strenuous. Fans at a baseball game often see players doing stretching exercises on the field before the game begins. A runner stretches the leg muscles and walks or jogs slowly before starting his or her run.

Warming up starts the lungs working harder to take in more oxygen. It starts the heart beating faster to send blood that contains oxygen flowing to the muscles. This prepares the muscles to begin working hard during strenuous exercise. Stretching makes muscles flexible and better able to do their work without injury. It also makes tendons flexible. Tendons connect muscles to bones. Ligaments hold bones together in joints, such as at the knee. Stretching the muscles around joints during a warm-up can prevent ligament injuries. A five-minute warm-up prepares the body for the vigorous activity ahead.

❯ When runners warm up, it is important for them to stretch the muscles at the back of the legs.

# Digging Deeper

## Your Challenge!

There are many benefits to warming up the body before exercise. To dig deeper into the issue:

Go online to find out more about different warm-up exercises and the benefits of each. Then, create a warm-up routine for yourself.

## Summary

A warm-up often improves a workout. Warming up increases the blood flow in muscles. Stretching keeps muscles flexible.

## Further Inquiry

Warming up is important for athletes of all ages. However, at different ages people may be more or less likely to be injured playing sports. Maybe we should ask:

**Are children more likely to get injured?**

Baseball warm-ups should include various stretching exercises. Baseball players use many different muscles during a game.

# Are Children More Likely to Get Injured?

At times, children and teenagers grow very quickly. These periods of rapid growth are called growth spurts. During growth spurts, a child or teenager's bones can grow faster than the muscles that make them move. This makes joints less flexible. As a result, young people have a greater chance of being injured playing sports. Children between the ages of 5 and 14 are most likely to experience such injuries.

Strains, sprains, and shin splints are some of the injuries that happen more often in growing children than in adults who play sports. A strain is an injury to a muscle or a tendon. In a sprain, a ligament becomes stretched or torn. Shin splints refers to pain along or just behind the shinbone in the lower leg.

⌄ Children can avoid some overuse injuries by warming up before playing a sport.

Strains, sprains, and shin splints are often caused by overuse of a body part. Overuse means working muscles and joints hard for long periods day after day. Knee problems and shin splints in long-distance runners are examples of overuse injuries. So are shoulder problems in baseball pitchers.

Scientists believe that a healthful balance of activities helps to prevent overuse injuries. Children should take at least one day a week off from playing sports. Before the teen years, athletes should not specialize in a single sport. Each sport puts the most stress on certain muscles and joints. By playing different sports, children allow some muscles to recover while they are using others.

# Digging Deeper

## Your Challenge!

Doctors and scientists think that many overuse injuries can be prevented. To dig deeper into the issue:

Research a common overuse injury in three different sports, not including running and baseball. Describe the causes and symptoms of each injury.

## Summary

Children are more likely than adults to get injured when they play sports. Sometimes, injuries happen because children's bones grow faster than their muscles.

## Further Inquiry

Sports injuries also happen to adults. Some sports put athletes at especially high risk of injury. Maybe we should ask:

**What are extreme sports?**

# What Are Extreme Sports?

Many athletes enjoy sports that allow them to be close to the natural environment. Some athletes even like the challenge of competing against features of the environment. They find the challenges they are looking for by taking part in extreme sports.

Extreme sports include rock climbing, skydiving, hang gliding, bungee jumping, mountain biking, and motocross. Athletes use special equipment to reach heights and speeds that would seem dangerous to most people. They may go into wilderness areas with rough terrain.

Rock climbers face the challenge of getting to the tops of cliffs and steep mountainsides. Skydivers, hang gliders, and bungee jumpers fly at or jump from great heights. Mountain bikers ride on rocky ground, up and down hills, for long distances. Motocross racers steer their motorcycles at high speed over rough off-road courses.

Some of the most extreme sporting events take place in the United States. In the Race Across America, athletes have 12 days to ride a bicycle across the United States. This is a distance of about 3,000 miles (4,800 kilometers). The Ironman World Championship takes place in Hawai'i. Athletes have to swim, bike, and run a footrace within 17 hours.

> White-water rafters enjoy the challenge of paddling down fast-flowing rivers.

> Rock climbing requires strength, fitness, and endurance. Climbers also need good judgment to help them pick the best route to the top.

# Digging Deeper

## Your Challenge!

Some athletes take part in extreme sports, which are more dangerous than other sports. To dig deeper into the issue:

Research an online or print interview with a person who takes part in an extreme sport. Find out what motivates the person to do what he or she does.

## Summary

Extreme sports are challenging activities in which athletes compete against nature or perform dangerous tasks. Some extreme sports are rock climbing, skydiving, and hang gliding.

## Further Inquiry

The dangerous challenges of extreme sports mean that athletes must be in very good shape, almost like machines. Maybe we should ask:

**What are human machines?**

# What Are Human Machines?

Scientists who study how the human body moves think of athletes' bodies as machines. One area of science looks at sports from a mechanical point of view. This area is called biomechanics. Using high-speed cameras and computer programs, scientists are able to analyze body movements in detail. They can see any problems with the way an athlete moves. Then, they can tell the athlete how to fix those problems to improve his or her performance.

One test in biomechanics uses a treadmill. Silver dots are attached to an athlete, such as a runner, at points along the body. These dots reflect light onto a high-speed camera. As the athlete runs on the treadmill, the camera takes pictures of the moving dots. A computer then analyzes the pictures. The computer program shows whether the athlete is running in the best way possible. It gives information about what can be done to improve performance. Even small changes in movement can make a difference in running speed. The test measures length of stride, foot placement, leg speed, and the way in which the athlete lifts his or her knees.

❯ A sports trainer can measure how much oxygen an athlete takes in with each breath. Then, the trainer can figure out how to help the athlete increase oxygen intake, which will improve performance.

# Digging Deeper

## Your Challenge!

Biomechanics can help athletes improve their performance. To dig deeper into the issue:

Research how athletes in three sports other than running use biomechanics to become better at what they do.

## Summary

Biomechanics treats the body as a machine. It uses technology to analyze athletes' movements.

## Further Inquiry

The human body can be considered a machine. Things outside the body can improve this machine's performance. Maybe we should ask:

**How does equipment help results?**

# How Does Equipment Help Results?

Athletes today have better equipment than ever before. For example, some new swimming pools are not as deep as older ones. A pool that is only 10 feet (3 m) deep reduces the downward waves created by swimmers' kicks. Swimmers go faster as a result.

Equipment created from synthetic, or human-made, materials has greatly improved results in many sports. Better equipment is one reason athletes often break sports records. In the first modern **Olympic Games** in 1896, the record pole vaulter reached a height of 10 feet, 10 inches (3.3 m) using a wooden pole. In 1940, Cornelius Warmerdan cleared 15 feet (4.5 m) using a bamboo pole. Today, using **fiberglass** poles, some athletes are able to vault more than 20 feet (6 m).

## 100-Meter Dash World Record Holders

### Women

| YEAR | ATHLETE | TIME |
|---|---|---|
| 1922 | Mary Lines | 12.8 seconds |
| 1932 | Hilda Strike | 11.9 seconds |
| 1961 | Wilma Rudolph | 11.2 seconds |
| 1982 | Marlies Gohr | 10.88 seconds |
| 1984 | Evelyn Ashford | 10.76 seconds |
| 1988 | Florence Griffith-Joyner | 10.49 seconds |

### Men

| YEAR | ATHLETE | TIME |
|---|---|---|
| 1912 | Donald Lippincott | 10.6 seconds |
| 1936 | Jesse Owens | 10.2 seconds |
| 1968 | Jim Hines | 9.99 seconds |
| 1991 | Carl Lewis | 9.86 seconds |
| 1999 | Maurice Greene | 9.79 seconds |
| 2009 | Usain Bolt | 9.58 seconds |

There have been many other improvements in sports equipment. At the 1996 Olympic Games, rowers pulled newly designed oars with hatchet-shaped blades that move more water. Softball players can hit balls farther with bats made from ultra-light metals, instead of wood. Tennis rackets are now made with fiberglass and light-weight metals. Today's tennis players can hit the ball at higher speeds than former players could with wooden rackets.

Divers now use boards that provide 15 percent more spring than diving boards that were used in the 1960s. Sprinters in races such as the 100-meter (328-feet) dash now press their heels against starting blocks at the beginning of a race. This gives them a faster start and shortens race times.

❯ Usain Bolt of Jamaica set the world record for the 100-meter dash at the 2009 World Championships in Berlin, Germany.

## Your Challenge!

Modern-day equipment has allowed athletes in many sports to perform better. To dig deeper into the issue:

Choose a sport not discussed here. Do research to find out how equipment has led to improved performances by athletes in that sport. Is today's equipment created from natural or human-made materials?

## Summary

From pools that allow swimmers to race faster to softball bats that allow players to hit farther, modern equipment has changed the way many sports are played.

## Further Inquiry

With so much improved equipment in sports, maybe we should ask:

### How does clothing affect performance?

# How Does Clothing Affect Performance?

The invention of new human-made materials used in clothing has had a large impact on sports. In addition to being comfortable to wear, these materials often help to improve an athlete's performance. Today's athletes also wear special clothing and equipment to help protect them from injury.

Many athletes, such as swimmers, runners, speed skaters, and bobsledders, wear spandex clothing. Spandex is a synthetic material that is thin, stretchable, and warm. It allows athletes to go faster because it reduces **friction** with the air or water as they move.

Some fabrics used in winter sports are waterproof and **breathable**. The outside layer of the fabric keeps out water. The inside layer allows sweat to evaporate, so that the body stays dry.

Helmets are worn in many sports. They protect the head in case the athlete suffers a fall, collides with another player, or is hit by a ball traveling at high speed. Safety glasses protect the eyes. They are worn in many court sports, such as squash and racquetball. Elbow pads and kneepads protect joints when people use in-line skates. Life jackets, worn during many water sports, have saved thousands of lives by preventing drowning.

⌄ Football helmets have padding to cushion the head and jaws of a player. The chin strap and face mask protect the chin and parts of the face.

## Your Challenge!

The clothing athletes wear can help them perform better in their sport. To dig deeper into the issue:

You will need a pencil, paper, stopwatch, and measuring tape. Measure 50 yards (46 m). Run the distance three times, wearing a different set of clothes each time. For the first run, wear a T-shirt, pants, a heavy coat, and boots. For the second run, wear a sweatshirt, pants, and street shoes. In the last run, wear a T-shirt, shorts, and running shoes. Record and compare your times. Which clothes helped to improve your running time?

## Summary

Athletes wear clothing that helps them be better at their sport.

## Further Inquiry

Scientists have wondered if athletes' fluid intake affects their performance. Maybe we should ask:

### Are sports drinks better than water?

# Are Sports Drinks Better Than Water?

Athletes need to drink liquids to prevent **dehydration**. When people sweat, their bodies lose water. If people lose too much water, they can suffer from fatigue and cramps. They may also be at risk of developing the serious medical problems heat exhaustion or heat stroke. Drinking water during and after exercise or while playing a sport is a good way to avoid dehydration.

When people sweat, their bodies also lose electrolytes. These are minerals that are very important to keep the body functioning well. Two of these minerals are sodium and potassium. Sodium helps the body hold on to water. Sodium and potassium are both necessary for nerves and muscles to work properly.

Sports drinks are products that contain water for rehydration, sugar for energy, and electrolytes to replace those lost in sweat. Sports drinks may be a better choice than plain water for **elite athletes** who are taking part in intense sports that last a long time. For example, long-distance runners may benefit from using sports drinks. If a person works out for fewer than 60 minutes, water is probably all he or she needs. The same is true for many people playing sports for fun.

❯ Drinking two to three glasses of water within two hours of exercising restores water the body lost from sweating.

# Digging Deeper

## Your Challenge!

Sports drinks contain a number of ingredients to help elite athletes. However, some people believe these drinks are used by too many athletes who do not need them. To dig deeper into the issue:

Research the arguments for and against the use of sports drinks by athletes not doing intense activity for a long time. Be sure to find at least one source that is for sports drinks and one that is against. Make a chart showing your findings.

## Summary

Athletes need to drink fluids in order to keep themselves hydrated.

## Further Inquiry

Taking in fluids is essential to athletes' health. Some athletes take in other things as well. Maybe we should ask:

### What are steroids?

⌃ Athletes who compete to win marathons may benefit from sports drinks.

# What Are Steroids?

Both professional and amateur athletes want to improve their strength and performance in sports. They want to be as strong and as fast as possible. Some people believe that taking drugs will help them become better athletes.

Some athletes take large doses of **anabolic steroids** in the hope of improving their performance. These drugs are similar to **hormones** that people produce naturally in their bodies in small amounts. Anabolic steroids stimulate muscles into taking in more **protein**. This leads to muscle growth. Steroids also may allow athletes to train harder by helping their muscles recover faster after a workout.

However, there are a number of problems connected with using steroids in sports. The drugs can cause liver damage, high blood pressure, and kidney problems. Steroid use can lead to heart attacks and strokes, even for athletes under the age of 30. The drugs can also affect a person's mood, making that person more aggressive and irritable. In addition, steroids give an athlete an unfair, unnatural advantage over his or her competitors.

❯ Cyclist Lance Armstrong admitted in 2013 that he had used drugs to help him win championships.

Some players, including Ryan Braun, have been suspended by Major League Baseball for using drugs that the league has banned.

# Digging Deeper

## Your Challenge!

Steroids have been banned by most professional sports organizations in the United States. To dig deeper into the issue:

Research steroids in the news. What actions have sports leagues and organizations taken recently to prevent steroid use by their players? Do you think such actions go far enough, not far enough, or too far in punishing athletes? Why?

## Summary

Some athletes take anabolic steroids in the hope of improving their performance. However, steroids have serious risks for the health of the athletes who take them.

## Further Inquiry

Using animals in a sport is a different way to change performance. Maybe we should ask:

**What role do animals play in sports?**

# What Role Do Animals Play in Sports?

People are not the only athletes. Even before chariots pulled by horses first circled arenas in ancient Rome, humans used animals in sports. In ancient Greece, Pakistan, and Africa, the sport of bull vaulting was popular. Cave paintings show that a person would catch a running bull by the horns. Then, the person would jump over the bull from front to back. Archaeologists, or scientists who study human life in the past, believe that either small adults or children took part in bull vaulting.

Large animals such as horses and bulls are still popular in sports. In North America, rodeos draw thousands of people each year. Cowboys test their skills at **bronc** riding, bull riding, steer wrestling, and calf roping. Horses are used in horse racing and polo.

In history and around the world today, people have used other animals besides horses in races. Sled-dog races are held in Alaska and other areas with cold climates. Greyhound racing is popular in parts of the United States and other countries. In South Africa, there are ostrich races.

A type of pigeon called a homing pigeon can be trained to return to its home when released from a distant place. In the ancient Olympic Games in Greece, homing pigeons carried messages with the results of events back to the athletes' home villages. When the modern Olympic Games started in 1896, pigeons were released at the beginning and ending ceremonies. That custom continues today.

^ The Iditarod Sled Dog Race takes place every winter in Alaska. Teams of sled dogs race more than 1,000 miles (1,600 km) across the frozen terrain.

# Digging Deeper

## Your Challenge!

Some people are concerned about the use of animals in sports. They are worried about the care and safety of the animals. To dig deeper into the issue:

Research an organization that works for animal rights. Summarize the position of the organization about the use of animals in sports. Then, decide how you feel about this position, and why.

## Summary

Horses, bulls, and dogs are just some of the animals used in sports today.

## Further Inquiry

In some sports, people move around on human-made equipment, rather than animals. Science helps this equipment to work properly. Maybe we should ask:

**How does a bike stay upright?**

# How Does a Bike Stay Upright?

Bicycle riders sometimes fall because their bikes tip over while they are riding. This often happens because the wheels are not turning fast enough to keep the bike moving forward. The wheels of a bicycle are two gyroscopes. A gyroscope is a spinning wheel mounted on a frame. When the wheel of a gyroscope is spinning, it resists any change in direction. This resistance keeps the bike stable and upright. The resistance to change increases as the wheel spins faster. As a result, the faster a rider travels in a straight direction, the less likely he or she is to tip over.

⌄The Tour de France is a three-week bike race that takes place every summer. Depending on their speed, riders take between 324,000 and 486,000 pedal strokes during the race.

⌃ Bicycle riders usually move more slowly on rough terrain than on smooth road surfaces. Both the slow speed and the bumps make falls more likely.

Many riders are especially likely to tip over when they are first learning to ride a bicycle. New riders may feel unsure of themselves. As a result, they tend to pedal slowly. As riders gain experience and begin to pedal faster, they are less likely to tip over.

## Your Challenge!

Why do some bicycles have wide tires, and other bikes have thinner tires? To dig deeper into the issue:

Research the kinds of tires used in different bicycle sports. Explain why wide tires are better for some sports and thin tires for others.

## Summary

A bicycle stays up when the rider is pedaling fast enough to keep the bicycle moving forward.

## Further Inquiry

When a bicycle is moving forward, it stays up due to the laws of physics. These laws may apply to other sports, such as surfing. Maybe we should ask:

**How do surfers stay on their boards?**

# How Do Surfers Stay on Their Boards?

Balance is important for many sports. In some sports, such as surfing, snowboarding, waterskiing, and skateboarding, balance is crucial. People who watch surfers riding the waves are sometimes amazed that these athletes are able to stand up on small, thin boards that are moving so quickly through the waves. With practice, however, surfers learn to keep their balance.

Maintaining balance is related to a person's center of **gravity**. Every person and object has a center of gravity. It is the point on which the object can be balanced. If one imagines trying to balance a person on the tip of a pin, the center of gravity is the one spot on the body where that can be done.

⌄ A surfer riding a wave uses his or her body to change the board's angle in the water. For example, moving toward the tail of the board will cause the board's nose to lift up.

In most men, the center of gravity is higher on the body than it is in most women. This is due to the fact that men tend to have wider and heavier shoulders. More of their weight is near the top of their bodies.

A surfer needs to know where his or her center of gravity is. For a surfer to stay on the board, that person's center of gravity must be over the board. If the athlete's center of gravity is not over the board, the surfer will fall off.

⌄ For snowboarders, keeping the center of gravity over the board is more difficult during turns.

## Your Challenge!

Surfers, skateboarders, and snowboarders must position their bodies properly over their boards. They must know about center of gravity. To dig deeper into the issue:

Perform a demonstration to find a center of gravity. Lay a pencil across an outstretched finger and try to balance it. The place where it balances perfectly is the pencil's center of gravity.

## Summary

In surfing and other sports, athletes rely on their center of gravity to continue standing as they move forward.

## Further Inquiry

Balance is essential to ice skaters, too. Maybe we should ask:

**Do ice skaters become dizzy when they spin?**

# Do Ice Skaters Become Dizzy When They Spin?

All people, including ice skaters, get dizzy from spinning. When a person stops spinning, the eyes tell the brain one thing, and the person's sense of balance tells the brain another. Ice skaters must learn how to solve this problem.

Balance is sensed by three tiny canals deep inside the ear. These canals are curled in loops and are filled with fluid. When the head or body starts moving or stops moving, the fluid pushes on tiny hairlike sensors in the canals. These sensors send a message to the brain, telling it what the body is doing.

When a person spins quickly and then stops, it takes time for the fluid in the ear to stop moving. This is the same effect as when water in a spinning cup continues to move for a few seconds after the cup has stopped. People feel dizzy because the brain is still receiving signals that say the body is spinning.

❯ After some very fast spins, a skater's eyes may move back and forth for a few seconds. This can make it harder for the skater to focus on an object and control dizziness.

To control their dizziness, ice skaters try to focus very quickly on a still object when they stop spinning. They also concentrate very hard while the brain sorts out some mixed messages. Doing these things helps the brain to adjust and the dizziness to go away more quickly.

## Your Challenge!

People first began to ice skate more than 4,000 years ago. Today, there are several sports in which athletes use ice skates. These sports include ice hockey, speed skating, ice dancing, and figure skating. To dig deeper into the issue:

Research several sports in which athletes use ice skates. Identify the sports in which dizziness is a problem. Why does it tend to occur in these sports and not the others?

## Summary

Dizziness can be a problem for skaters who spin quickly. They learn to overcome dizziness by focusing on an object that is not moving.

## Further Inquiry

In skating, an athlete spins. In baseball, the pitcher makes a ball spin. Maybe we should ask:

**How does a pitcher outsmart a batter?**

# How Does a Pitcher Outsmart a Batter?

A good baseball pitcher knows how to put different spins on a ball to make the batter swing and miss, rather than hit the ball. The pitcher knows how to throw a ball so that it curves in a direction the batter cannot predict. A ball spinning through the air is affected by the laws of **aerodynamics**. Types of spin used by baseball pitchers include underspin, overspin, and sidespin.

As a ball spins, it is surrounded by a layer of air. The stitches on a baseball, the dimples on a golf ball, and the fuzz on a tennis ball help to grab hold of this layer of air. The way an athlete throws or hits a ball will determine its spin. That spin is also affected by different movements of air acting on the ball.

The movement of a ball in the air can be compared to the water that is churned up in a V shape behind a moving boat. This is called a wake. When a ball moves through the air, the same thing happens, except that the wake behind a baseball is made up of air and is invisible.

❯ By the time it reaches the batter, a pitch with spin can move as much as 18 inches (46 centimeters) from a straight line.

## Types of Spin

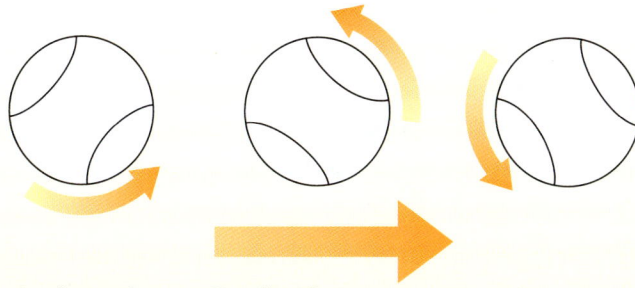

### Underspin, or Backspin

Underspin, or backspin, produces faster-moving air on top of the ball and slower-moving air under the ball. This combination pulls the ball upward.

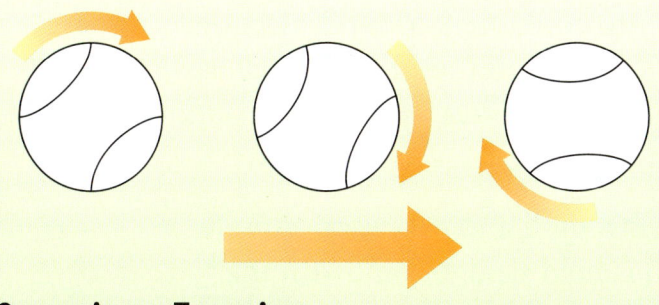

### Overspin, or Topspin

Overspin, or topspin, produces faster-moving air under the ball. This pulls the ball downward.

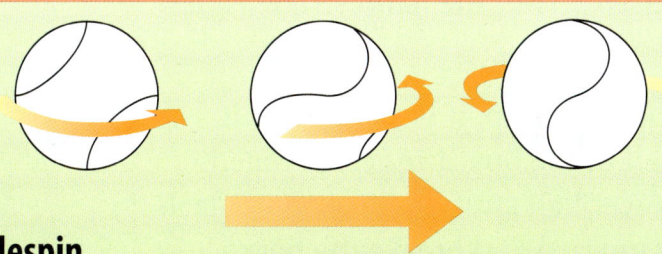

### Sidespin

With sidespin, air is moving faster across one side of the ball, which makes the ball move sideways. This is the most unpredictable pitch that can be thrown.

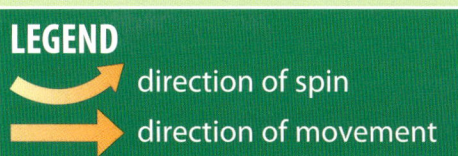

**LEGEND**
→ direction of spin
→ direction of movement

# Digging Deeper

## Your Challenge!

The laws of aerodynamics determine the movement of objects through air. To dig deeper into the issue:

Run across a field with a large sheet of cardboard held in front of you, or ride a bicycle into the wind. How does the cardboard or the wind affect your movement? Do research to find out why this effect happens.

## Summary

A baseball pitcher uses spin to affect the movement of the ball as it heads toward the batter.

## Further Inquiry

In baseball, a pitcher relies on principles of aerodynamics to outsmart the other team's batters. A different scientific principle is at work in the sport of karate. Maybe we should ask:

**How can a karate chop break a board?**

# How Can a Karate Chop Break a Board?

It is hard to imagine how a karate chop from a human hand can break a thick wooden board, or several boards at once. However, when a powerful force is concentrated on a small area, this is exactly what happens. Breaking a board with a single blow also requires a great deal of practice.

Karate masters are people who have expert skills and long experience in the sport. As part of their training, they toughen their hands by pushing them into containers of sand, rice, or gravel. This causes calluses to develop on their hands. Calluses are areas of hard and thickened skin. Calluses protect the hand during a blow and can also increase the force of the blow.

Karate masters put all of their strength and concentration into the blow. Often, the hand is held straight out, with the side of the hand opposite the thumb facing downward. This is called a knife position, Sometimes, the hand is curled into a fist, known as a hammer position. The karate chop must be thrown quickly and precisely. After the hand strikes, it is pulled back instantly.

When the board is hit by a karate chop, it bends before it breaks in two. The upper half of the board squeezes together under the blow, while the lower half stretches apart and starts to crack. The crack spreads upward and breaks the board.

A stack of boards to be broken by a karate chop is called pegged if there are spaces between the boards.

# Digging Deeper

## Your Challenge!

A karate chop is one of the most powerful movements in sports. To dig deeper into the issue:

Research what happens when karate chops are applied to other objects besides boards. What laws of science cause these objects to break?

## Summary

In karate, athletes apply a great deal of force in a highly concentrated way. They can even break concrete blocks with their bare hands.

## Further Inquiry

A karate chop shows the power of concentrated force. A boomerang illustrates another physical force. Maybe we should ask:

**What makes a boomerang return?**

# What Makes a Boomerang Return?

Boomerangs were invented by Australian Aborigines thousands of years ago. They were originally used as weapons for hunting small birds. Today, people throw boomerangs for fun, or they may compete to see who can throw one the farthest. Boomerang throwing is a worldwide sport. The United States Boomerang Association holds tournaments every year, including a national championship.

Boomerangs are thin and have a V shape. They are often made out of wood. There are two kinds of boomerangs. The nonreturning boomerang is heavier and larger, measuring 24 to 36 inches (60 to 90 cm) long. It has been used to hunt large game, such as kangaroos, and also as a weapon in war.

The returning boomerang is about 12 to 30 inches (30 to 75 cm) long. One side is flat, and the other side is slightly curved, much like the wing of an airplane. The boomerang is held vertically in the throwing hand, with the flat part in the palm of the hand. When it is thrown, the boomerang moves forward and also spins.

As a returning boomerang is moving, the air on its curved side becomes thinner. The denser air on the flat side creates a force that constantly pushes the boomerang sideways. This is why the boomerang will travel in a curving path that will bring it back to the thrower.

In some boomerang competitions, points are awarded for unusual catches. These include the under-the-leg catch and the foot catch.

A person throwing a returning boomerang should release it from his or her hand at eye height.

# Digging Deeper

## Your Challenge!

Boomerangs travel as they do because of the same scientific principle that applies to airplane wings and helicopter propellers. To dig deeper into the issue:

Research why airplanes and helicopters are able to get off the ground. In what position do the wings or helicopter blades have to be for this to happen?

## Summary

There are two types of boomerangs. Returning boomerangs must have a certain shape in order to fly in a curved path.

## Further Inquiry

The laws of science affect other moving objects in sports. Maybe we should ask:

### Why do balls bounce?

# Why Do Balls Bounce?

A ball being held above the ground has the potential to fall toward Earth if the person holding it lets go. For this reason, the ball is said to have potential, or stored, energy. When the ball is released, gravity starts pulling it down. As the ball falls, its stored energy changes into **kinetic energy**. When the ball hits the ground, its movement stops and it becomes slightly flattened. Its kinetic energy changes into potential energy once again. As the ball returns to its original shape, the potential energy changes back into kinetic energy, and the ball bounces upward.

‹ The speed at which a tennis ball is hit also affects the height of its bounce. The fastest recorded speed of a tennis ball serve was 163 miles (263 km) per hour.

Energy cannot disappear. It can only change from one form into another, such as from potential to kinetic energy. However, most balls do not bounce back as high as they were dropped. This is because not all of the potential energy the ball has when it hits the ground changes back into kinetic energy. Some turns into heat energy as the ball rubs against the ground. Some also changes into sound energy. That is why you hear a noise when a ball hits the ground.

The amount of energy that can be stored by a ball depends on what the ball is made of. For example, a rubber tennis ball can store more energy than a leather baseball. This helps explain why a tennis ball bounces higher than a baseball if both are dropped from the same height.

⌄ A soccer player's kick gives kinetic energy to the soccer ball.

# Digging Deeper

## Your Challenge!

When a ball bounces, energy changes from one form to another. To dig deeper into the issue:

Research other events in sports in which energy changes form. For example, what happens when a baseball player slides into a base? For the action you select, what kind of energy was there at the beginning of the play? What forms of energy did it change into at the end of the play?

## Summary

A ball bounces when its potential energy becomes kinetic energy, heat energy, and sound energy.

## Further Inquiry

Fully understanding the connection between sports and science has involved asking many questions and researching many issues. Taking all we have learned, maybe we finally can answer:

## What is a sport?

# Putting It All Together

There are many different kinds of sports, but they all share some features. First, each sport follows a set of rules. Second, athletes need good physical abilities and training to do well in sports. Finally, science has an important role in sports.

Advancements in science have affected sports performance over time. Technology has made better equipment possible in sports such as swimming, softball, and track and field. The use of human-made materials in sports clothing has improved performance in sports such as speed skating and bobsledding.

## The Science of Sports

In addition to being governed by rules, sports are governed by science. The laws of biology explain why we breathe harder and sweat during exercise. They explain why warming up before exercise is important. The laws of chemistry clarify the difference between sports drinks and water. They also explain the dangers of using steroids. The laws of physics are at work in many sports. They account for why a ball bounces and why a baseball spins. They explain why a boomerang returns and how surfers stay on their boards. Understanding the science of sports helps people become better athletes and enjoy playing their favorite sports.

⌃The laws of science explain why the type of fabric used to make a swimsuit can help the swimmer race faster.

# Sports Careers

## Coach

Someone who likes sports and enjoys working with other people may want to become a coach. A coach helps athletes train, practice, and become better at whatever sport they play. He or she may decide on the best physical training program for a given sport. A coach also works with an athlete during practice. The coach helps the athlete learn how to move in the best way. For team sports, the coach decides which players will play. The coach also gives the team strategies to help win the game.

## Sports Medicine Specialist

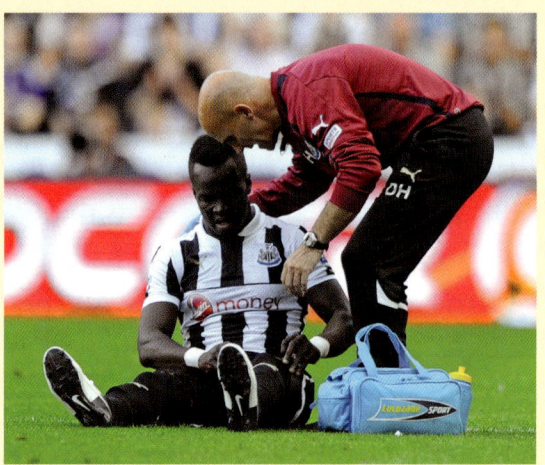

Sports medicine is the branch of medicine that helps athletes stay healthy and deals with sports injuries. People who are interested in biology, medicine, sports, and working with other people may find that sports medicine is a good career choice. Sports medicine specialists include doctors, physical therapists, trainers, and other health care workers. Trainers help athletes build physical fitness to improve their skills. Trainers also work with athletic teams and provide first aid to injured players. Sports psychologists help athletes develop a good mental outlook and overcome stress.

# Young Scientists at Work

Salt water is denser than fresh water because it contains dissolved salt. How does the presence of salt in water affect the ability of objects to float?

## Materials

One small glass
One large glass
Measuring cup
Tap water
Measuring spoons
Salt
Two uncooked eggs

## Instructions

1. Fill the small glass with 1 cup (250 milliliters) of tap water.

2. Make salt water by using 1 cup (250 mL) of warm or hot water from the tap. Then, add 2 tablespoons (30 mL) of salt. Stir until all of the salt is dissolved.

3. Fill the large glass about half full with salt water.

4. Gently place one egg in the glass that has fresh water.

5. Place the other egg in the glass that has salt water.

6. Remove the egg from the fresh-water glass. Pour some of the fresh water into the salt-water glass, adding it gently down the inside of the glass. Keep adding water slowly.

## Observations

What happened to the two eggs when you put one in the fresh-water glass and one in the salt-water glass?

What happened to the egg in the salt-water glass when you added fresh water to that glass?

How does this experiment relate to swimming?

# Quiz

How healthy are you? Do you think you are as fit as you can be? Young people need regular exercise, good food, and a great deal of sleep in order to stay healthy and grow strong.

Most growing children need 60 minutes or more of moderate exercise each day. How often do you exercise or play sports? What exercise or sports do you do? How long do you play?

The U.S. government's food guide says people need six servings of grain products each day, two servings of fruit, three servings of vegetables, two servings of milk products, and two servings of meat or other foods with a great deal of protein. What types of food do you eat each day?

Most children need to drink about 7 to 8 cups (1.7 to 1.9 liters) of water a day. How much water do you drink?

Young people need at least 8 to 10 hours of sleep each night. How much sleep do you get?

# Key Words

**aerodynamics:** the branch of science that studies the movement of objects through air

**anabolic steroids:** synthetic hormones that are taken to increase the size of muscles

**biology:** the branch of science that deals with living things and the ways they grow and function

**breathable:** allowing air to pass through

**bronc:** a horse that has not been trained to carry human riders

**cells:** the smallest structures that make up all living things

**chemistry:** the branch of science that deals with the structure of substances and how they react under various conditions

**dehydration:** the loss of an abnormally high amount of body fluids

**elite athletes:** athletes who compete at the highest level in their sport

**endurance:** the ability to do something for a long time

**evaporates:** changes from a liquid into a gas

**fiberglass:** a light, strong, and flexible material made of glass fibers

**friction:** a force that causes a person or object to slow down as a result of rubbing against something

**gravity:** a force that pulls objects toward the center of Earth

**hormone:** a substance produced in the body that affects the way the body grows or functions

**kinetic energy:** energy that an object has because it is in motion

**Olympic Games:** an international sports competition held every four years

**physics:** the branch of science dealing with matter, energy, motion, and the ways they work together

**protein:** a substance found especially in meats, eggs, beans, and dairy products that is important to the growth of body cells

**tissue:** a collection of cells of the same type that makes up structures in the body

# Index

aerodynamics 34, 35
animals in sports 26, 27
athlete 4, 5, 6, 13, 14, 16, 18, 20, 22, 24, 30, 31, 34, 42, 43, 44

balance 30, 31, 32
biomechanics 16, 17

clothing 20, 21, 42

electrolytes 22, 23
energy 8, 9, 22, 40, 41
equipment 14, 18, 19, 20, 42
extreme sports 14, 15

gravity 30, 31, 40

injuries 10, 12, 13, 14

minerals 22
muscles 4, 5, 6, 7, 8, 9, 10, 12, 13, 24

Olympic Games 18, 19, 27
oxygen 8, 9, 10

sports drinks 22, 23, 43
steroids 24, 25, 43

# Log on to www.av2books.com

AV² by Weigl brings you media enhanced books that support active learning. Go to www.av2books.com, and enter the special code found on page 2 of this book. You will gain access to enriched and enhanced content that supplements and complements this book. Content includes video, audio, weblinks, quizzes, a slide show, and activities.

## AV² Online Navigation

**Audio**
Listen to sections of the book read aloud.

**Video**
Watch informative video clips.

**Book Pages**
AV² pages directly correspond to pages in the book.

**Embedded Weblinks**
Gain additional information for research.

**Key Words**
Study vocabulary, and complete a matching word activity.

**Try This!**
Complete activities and hands-on experiments.

**Quizzes**
Test your knowledge.

**Slide Show**
View images and captions, and prepare a presentation.

AV² was built to bridge the gap between print and digital. We encourage you to tell us what you like and what you want to see in the future.

## Sign up to be an AV² Ambassador at www.av2books.com/ambassador.

Due to the dynamic nature of the Internet, some of the URLs and activities provided as part of AV² by Weigl may have changed or ceased to exist. AV² by Weigl accepts no responsibility for any such changes. All media enhanced books are regularly monitored to update addresses and sites in a timely manner. Contact AV² by Weigl at 1-866-649-3445 or av2books@weigl.com with any questions, comments, or feedback.